To Hiro,
   You have lots of great ideas! Here is a place to keep track of them. Remember... no idea is a bad idea. Every good invention needs to start somewhere!
      NEVER stop inventing!
                        Love,
                        Tadashi

Hiro's Journal

IF FOUND, PLEASE RETURN ASAP TO:
Hiro Hamada

studio fun BOOKS

White Plains, New York • Montréal, Québec • Bath, United Kingdom

My own journal!
Where do I start?
What do I write?
I guess I can start with
my most recent invention:
hover-cat boots.
Been tweaking them for
months.

   Mochi wasn't into it
at first. But now he's a pro!
   The key is to relax your cat.
I think he kinda likes
being a hover-cat!

This is me and Moc[...]
before we both ma[...]
history!

   Tadashi was a little freaked out when
Mochi first hovered above his head.

Putting boots on a cat:
1. Scratch cat's chin
2. Gently caress his paws
3. Slip boots on paws 1 and 2
4. On paw 3, stop; scratch
   chin again; repeat.
      (this is important)
VOILA! HOVER-CAT!

I was able to capture Tadashi's first reaction with my bedroom cam. This was right before he jumped out of bed... and accidentally broke my camera.

Each boot is 1 3/4" of pure awesomeness!

Next step is to develop human-sized hover-boots!

SAN FRANSOKYO INSTITUTE OF TECHNOLOGY

NAME
Tadashi Hamada

FORM CLASS
11D

STUDENT ID
00640

Tadashi "lost" his school ID today. Looks like I "found" it!

CHECK OUT THE HOVER-CART!
This is where I got the idea for Mochi's boots!

Tadashi + Hiro = ~~WORLD~~ UNIVERSE-changing technology!

Tadashi and I used to make tons of inventions together. But there is less time for that now. He decided to go to San Fransokyo Institute of Technology, aka SFIT. Boring! Sure, it's one of the most elite technology schools in the world. But it's not for me. I have other plans. Bot-fighting for one.

My robot is the best in town. It can beat anyone else's robot in the fighting ring. Anytime. Anywhere.

Introducing: MEGABOT! Baddest bot in San Fransokyo. He might not look like much, but he is a powerhouse!

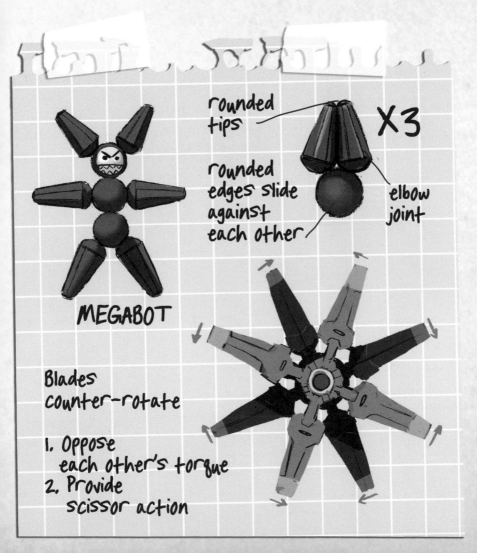

rounded tips

X3

rounded edges slide against each other

elbow joint

MEGABOT

Blades counter-rotate

1. Oppose each other's torque
2. Provide scissor action

Usually, I don't mind working in Aunt Cass's coffee shop. But today she made Tadashi and me work a longer shift.

It's not so bad, I guess. After all, I can always use some spare change to buy bot materials.

But how much coffee can people DRINK??

Time to automate! Presenting the Hamada Caffeination Delivery System:

arm with stabilizers to prevent spills

Cup-holder with pressure-sensors to prevent crushing

rubberized tips on the wheels allow for slipless movement

No more trips back and forth to the coffee machine! Yeah!

Tadashi says if we get our drink delivery system out there we will never have to work again! (Okay, so we will work LESS, maybe not NEVER.)

That's fine with me. More time for bot-fighting and perfecting my robot technology!

Zipbot

Dino Mechbot

My family is pretty cool!

Bunny ears?! And Tadashi calls ME "knucklehead!"

I can't BELIEVE it!

Aunt Cass gave us the garage today. I mean, she did not really "give" the garage to us, but she helped set it up so that we can work there.

Okay, actually, the garage is to help Tadashi. It's kind of his lab, where he can work on his technology homework from SFIT. Lucky for me, I get to use the space, too.

I am going to make so many robots here!

Bot fight here

and here

RIP
Little Yama!

Speaking of bots, there are lots of fights coming up.

Competition is fierce. But you can't let them see you sweat. And SOME people take it very seriously. Especially when they are beat by a kid.

Yama (who is 500 pounds) hadn't lost a bot fight. Ever. Until he met my bot. I think I need to stay away from his part of town for a while if I want to see my 15th birthday!

Won 3 fights in a row!
DO NOT RETURN
FOR 3 MONTHS.

Bot fight
here

Undefeated!

New bot fight
here. Starting
when??

So many bot fights...so little time...

I finally gave in and visited SFIT with Tadashi today. He's been dying to show me around. My brother is practically a walking banner for the place (IF he puts on the T-shirt, the hat, and the sweats all at once). So I went.

It turns out the place is seriously AWESOME.

I feel like I belong there! RIGHT NOW!

Tadashi took me to the SFIT Robotics lab, I have never seen anything like it!!

And there's this one professor dude (Professor Callaghan?) who is super smart. He seemed pretty impressed with my battle bot.

Tadashi says there's a tech showcase coming up. If I create the best tech, I'm in!!

I HAVE TO WIN!

Goal: Get into SFIT

what is THE best tech
I can create?

While I was at SFIT, I also saw Tadashi's friends and got to see what they are working on. They're all inventing new technology. It's incredible! And they have super cool names: Wasabi, Honey, and Go Go. I have to admit, they are pretty awesome!

Then there is this guy, Fred. He is the only one in the group who is not some science/tech genius. He doesn't go to SFIT, but he is their mascot and hangs out on campus all the time. Makes sense since he loves costumes (especially wearing them!). He's totally obsessed with comics.

In my spare time:

Build a remote-control Kaiju for Fred. Accept Fred's praise and undying loyalty!

The gang: Honey, Wasabi, Tadashi, Fred, and Go Go!

Wasabi is a NEAT FREAK! His workstation is impeccable. Not a speck of dirt or clutter in sight. He'd flip out if he saw my bedroom! He says he has a "system." Seems to be working for him.

It's pretty obvious that Wasabi is brilliant. He's created the world's most precise laser. He gave me a demonstration. He threw an apple in the air and as it fell, it was sliced into HUNDREDS of perfect thin slices. Never seen anything like it.
It's HALF A MICRON wide!

NOTE: Ask Wasabi about using the laser.

Remember Wasabi's rules:
"A place for everything.
Everything in its place."

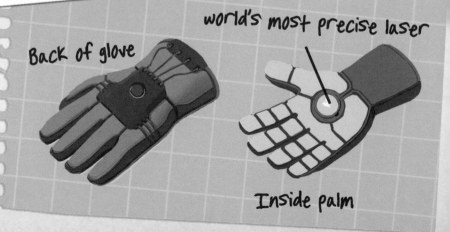

world's most precise laser

Back of glove

Inside palm

Honey does not look at all like a chemistry geek. But she is. She turned 400 POUNDS of tungsten carbide into dust—DUST!

She's really into chemistry. Chemistry's cool, but not as great as robotics. She's developed chemical concoctions that do everything from creating light to melting pure steel. She's even come up with a foam that hardens immediately on contact.

Somehow, everything ends up very colorful.

Today's concoction was PINK.

BLECH.

chemical foam

hardens on contact

Honey is as sweet as her name!

Go Go doesn't talk much, but somehow she gets her point across. And that girl loves moving fast. Not only that, Go Go knows every shortcut there is in the city! It's like she has a map in her brain! Plus, she is not scared of ANYTHING.

The day I visited SFIT, Go Go was working on a big project—a superfast bike that folds into a little case for portability. Did I mention that it has

NO BRAKES?

Go Go doesn't need them. She hardly ever stops!

Go Go is
SO COOL!
I hope I get to try out her bike one day.

Go Go and her bike. Ready to ride!

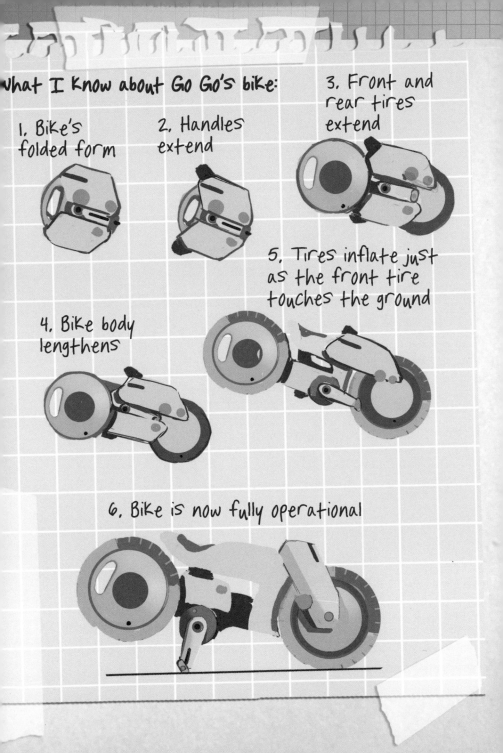

Tadashi has been working REALLY HARD on his project for robotics class. Today, I actually got to SEE it.

It is INCREDIBLE.

At first, I didn't think it was cool, but it can do some amazing things. It's a nurse bot named BAYMAX.

This bot actually almost seems to care. It's the way Tadashi programmed him:

1) Baymax hears a distress sound from a human and activates.
2) Human reports pain on a scale.
3) Baymax scans human using his hyperspectral cameras. That's pretty advanced stuff!
4) Baymax diagnoses problem. (HE HAS A HUGE DATABASE!)
5) Robot gives treatment! His nurse chip has 10,000 medical procedures!
6) Human is happy— TADASHI RULES!!!

I think he was inspired to build Baymax by all our trips to the emergency room growing up. Inventing flying things can be dangerous!

I saw this sketch of Baymax in the garbage and couldn't leave it there. IT IS SO COOL!

Baymax is BIG and would not be easy to store around the house. But my brother is always thinking and gave him an incredible design. Baymax fits into a little portable suitcase!!! When he's needed, he inflates like a balloon until he's full-size. When he's finished doing his job, he deflates back into his case. My brother is amazing!

I HAVE to create something awesome spectacular for the Showcase. I have so many ideas of things I want to invent and SFIT is the prime place to do it. AND I'd get to work with my brother. It's win/WIN!

My battle bots can wait for now.

It's time to get to work!

Another treasure from Tadashi's trash!!!!

Baymax portable case, Prototype 14

Arm rotates at the shoulder - hand reveals sucker

It's really late and I can barely keep my eyes open. I've been working non-stop on my project for the Showcase. I am creating tiny robots.

I call them MICROBOTS.

By themselves, they are kinda wimpy, but when they swarm together, they can make ANY SHAPE. The best part? I control them WITH MY MIND! I'm developing a headband to do this. I have lots of ideas for applications!

skateboard

robotic digger

Didn't get much any sleep last night. Too excited. I am totally psyched about the Showcase. Tadashi thought it would be a good idea to bring my journal with me to help keep me focused and so I can write down any ideas that I might get from seeing the tech there. I am at the Showcase RIGHT NOW!

The day so far is already awesome. I just saw Alistair Krei—the most famous alumnus of SFIT!! He started Krei Tech, and it's the best, biggest, most AMAZING tech company in the world. And he's at the Showcase LOOKING FOR NEW TECH!

This could be the biggest day of my life!!!!!!

People have some interesting ideas. Right now there is a guy presenting self-cleaning underwear! Not a bad idea!

SAN FRANSOKYO INSTITUTE OF TECHNOLOGY

SFIT SHOWCASE

SPONSORED BY KREI TECH INDUSTRIES

ANNUAL SFIT
TECHNOLOGY SHOWCASE

SCHEDULE OF EVENTS

8:00	EXHIBITOR SIGN-IN
9:00	WELCOME FROM ALISTAIR KREI
9:30-4:00	SHOWCASE FLOOR OPEN
11:00-2:00	EXHIBITOR DEMONSTRATIONS
4:00	AWARD CEREMONY
5:00	RECEPTION

Everyone has such great ideas! We saw robotic dog walkers, glow-in-the dark cement, and rain-clouds-on-demand!

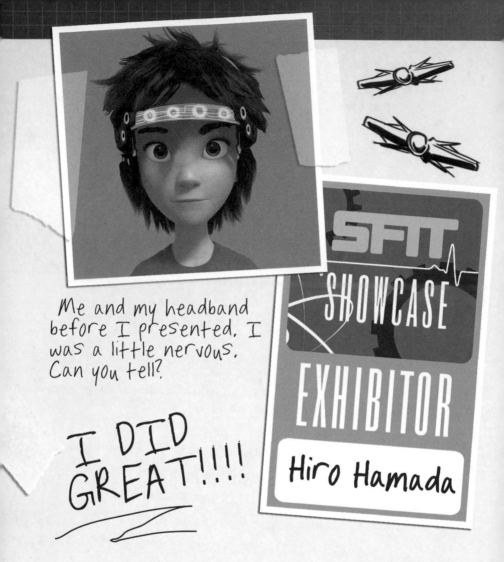

Me and my headband before I presented. I was a little nervous. Can you tell?

I DID GREAT!!!!

SFIT

SHOWCASE

EXHIBITOR

Hiro Hamada

They loved me! My microbots were fully functional, and my neurocranial transmitter worked perfectly.

I got a standing ovation.

AND I GOT INTO SFIT! YEAH!

I had to sneak off and write this.
Alistair Krei wanted to buy the microbots.
He offered me tons of money. It was
tempting, but I decided to turn him down.

Professor Callaghan seems to think that
Krei doesn't practice sound science. Plus,
I think the Hamada brothers can change
the ~~world~~ universe on our own. After all,
we will soon be making TONS of high-
tech, money-making creations!

I'm gonna go celebrate with
Tadashi and his friends. I can't
wait to start classes!

R.I.P. Tadashi I miss you

I just can't believe it.
Tadashi is gone.

Forever.

I'm DONE with
this journal and DONE with
inventing. What's the point?
Aunt Cass keeps coming to
the room, reminding me to eat,
get out of bed, and maybe go to
school. School is the LAST
place I want to go.

I wish everyone would just
leave me alone.

why? why?

why?

SFIT Blast Kills Two

An explosion yesterday at San Fransokyo Institute of Technology claimed the lives of Professor Robert Callaghan and student Tadashi Hamada. Both men had just attended the annual SFIT Showcase at the university where there were hundreds in attendance.

Eyewitnesses reported that most of the Showcase attendees had departed the showcase hall when a fire broke out. Several SFIT personnel and students tried to extinguish the fire, but it spread too quickly. They left the building and

were treated for smoke-inhalation and released.

Bystanders reported that Hamada ran into the burning building when he realized that Professor Callaghan was still inside the showcase hall. Shortly after Hamada entered the building, a loud explosion shook the grounds.

The cause of the fire remains unknown and is considered suspicious. It is currently under investigation by the San Fransokyo Fire Department. Alistair Krei, the founder and CEO of Krei Tech Industries could not be reached for comment.

~~Today was like all the other days~~

~~Been sleeping a lot, my friends are~~

Today, I actually feel like writing. I have something to write about. I hurt my toe and Baymax inflated. I totally forgot about him. HE STILL WORKS!!

But...he's kind of annoying. He's SUPER pushy and is obsessed with giving me a puberty diagnosis.

THAT is what he came up with after I hurt my TOE!!! And I didn't even want him to scan me anyway!!

CREEPY

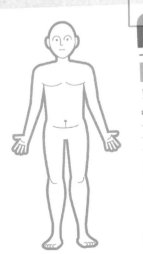

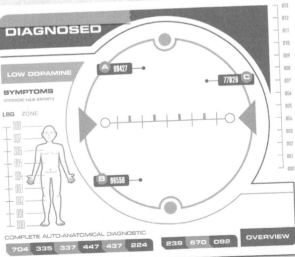

DIAGNOSED

LOW DOPAMINE

SYMPTOMS
SPORADIC HAIR GROWTH

LBG ZONE

COMPLETE AUTO-ANATOMICAL DIAGNOSTIC

704 335 337 447 437 224   239 670 092   OVERVIEW

A 99427   77828 C

B 96558

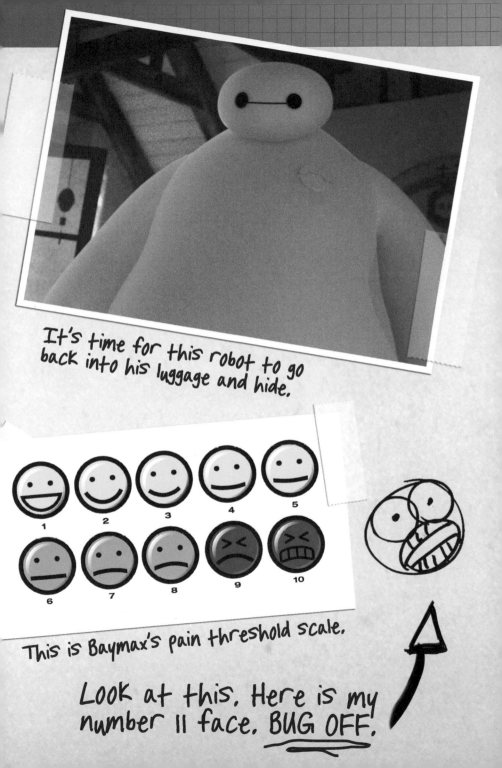

It's time for this robot to go back into his luggage and hide.

This is Baymax's pain threshold scale.

LOOK at this. Here is my number 11 face. BUG OFF.

Something else weird happened.

I found a microbot. In my room! This is strange. I thought the microbots were all destroyed in the explosion. The weird thing is that it's functioning...it shouldn't be working without the rest. It's going NUTS! I'm watching it vibrate all over the place. I am not controlling it, and no one else is controlling it (obviously). I think it's broken.

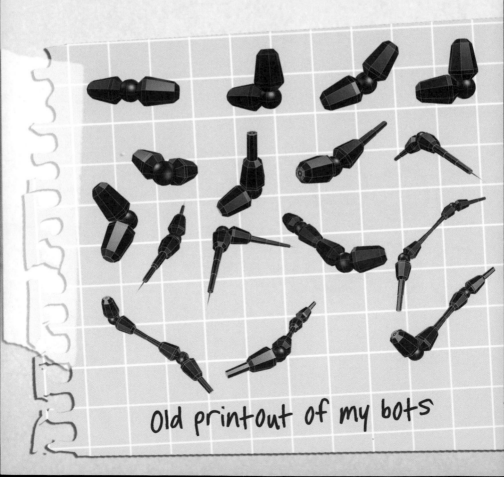

Old printout of my bots

Help me! Help me! I'm going crazy! where are my friends?!

Dumb microbot.

I put it in a petri dish to keep it from bouncing under the bed or something. I just want to go to sleep. Baymax seems pretty interested in it.

GOTTA RUN. I just saw Baymax running down the street! WHERE IS HE GOING?

I'm back.
Today was UNBELIEVABLE.

I finally caught up with Baymax at an old abandoned warehouse on the other side of town.
The microbot was still going crazy, so we decided to go in, but the only way in was through a window.
Once I unstuck Baymax from the window (robot needs a diet, ASAP) we made our way inside. Then I heard a SOUND. And what I saw made my hair stand on end.

SOMEONE is building ~~hundreds~~ thousands of microbots! I saw them with my own eyes and it was STILL hard to believe! Then I saw him. Some dude wearing a horrifying Kabuki mask. He looked like a bad guy out of Fred's comics. And he was coming for US!

who IS this guy??.

Baymax and I barely got
out with all our arms and legs. Looks like
the masked man has figured out a way to
control my microbots...with his mask.
He made them go nuts and
attack us!
This is SO out of control. I am going to
the police. We need help with this.

BAD news: Baymax almost deflated right there in the police station. To make matters worse, he was acting like a crazy person because of his low battery.

TERRIBLE news: The police didn't believe my story. I could not be more frustrated!!!

NO ONE IS GOING TO HELP WITH THIS. I'm on my own. I gotta get Baymax home to fix him.

I barely made it into the house without Aunt Cass noticing. Baymax was wobbling around, and slurring his words. He almost gave us away. I put him in his charger.

Then he said something: "Tadashi"

I had to explain to him that Tadashi was killed in a fire. He tried to tell me Tadashi lives in my heart. People keep saying that, but he's gone and nothing will change that.

Baymax can't fix it. But he tried.

He changed my diagnosis from "puberty" to "personal loss." Then he gave me the treatment—a hug. Tadashi knew what he was doing when he programmed Baymax. The hug really did make me feel better...it was almost like a part of Tadashi was with me just then. I miss him so much.

Went to the police and all I got were these stupid stickers!

Now that I've had more time to think,
I realize things have gone from bad to
SUPERbad.

THE FIRE AT SFIT
WASN'T AN ACCIDENT!!

How did I not think of this before???
The guy in the mask...HE must have set
the fire at the school. It was a way
to steal my microbots without anyone
noticing.

That means
HE is responsible
for Tadashi—
the reason
Tadashi died.

I know what I
need to do.

New Project:

Baymax needs to be more like my battle bots. He is strong, but his vinyl rips too easily. I bet I can come up with some armor. And maybe add another computer chip. One that teaches him to fight! I will do it. For Tadashi.

arm plates

head gear

chest plate

shoulder pads

chip access

flex plates

flex plates

Leg plates

metal boot

WOOT! I did it!

Baymax is ready for action! The armor isn't pretty. It's pretty goofy, actually, but it will do the job. I also successfully programmed a fighting chip. I put it inside his chest next to Tadashi's nurse chip. Then it was time to see what he could do.

Baymax was impressive to watch! He was used to being a big, huggable nurse bot. Fighting was not even in his vocabulary. But then I had an idea. I told him I would FEEL BETTER if he practiced his fighting moves. It worked! Baymax agreed! Now, with his armor and his karate moves,

Baymax ROCKS.

Hiiiiiii-YYYYAYYAYA!!

One day, I taught Baymax what a fist bump was. He totally didn't get it at first. He thought it was another fight move. Then he added it to his care-giving matrix...and he is doing it to everyone! Hahaha, I may have created a monster!

Okay, signing out. On our way to the warehouse to face the masked guy and

show him what we've got!

Puberty can often be a confusing time for a young adolescent flowering into manhood.

An oldie, but goodie!

WOW! Things are heating up! Me and my friends were almost KILLED tonight!!!!

Oh, MAN. It's hard to think straight.

The warehouse was empty. Baymax and I followed my microbot to a pier. Then, the masked creepy dude showed up. He was pretty ~~hard~~ IMPOSSIBLE to miss. He was riding a wave of thousands—no— MILLIONS of microbots. My microbots! My amazing microbots are under the control of a madman!

What have I done? I've created millions of little monsters. I wish I had never invented them.

I have to fix this.

The microbots were carrying the masked dude and a giant object. No idea what it is. For all I know, it's a giant microbot...or a MACROBOT!

It's REALLY nice to have friends. The ones that watch your back. Friends like mine.

Without them, Baymax and I would have been microbot chop meat. Toast.

Tonight, my friends showed up in the nick of time in Wasabi's car. The masked man was using my microbots in an all-out attack! He tried to crush us with a giant shipping container.

Next thing I knew, Go Go was dragging me to the car and we were off driving through the streets of San Fransokyo! The crazy masked guy was in hot pursuit.

Then we were IN the bay. Trapped in our car under the water. You can't make this stuff up. Seriously.

That's when I realized that having a giant marshmallow bubble bot is not so bad. Baymax took his armor off so he could float us to the surface. He SAVED us!

After that, Fred took us all home—to his MANSION! It was like stepping into an alternate reality. How could we not know Fred is FILTHY RICH?! CRAZY RICH! $$$

Fred always looks like he just woke up! And like he lives under a bridge.

Fred has a butler, Heathcliff. Most awesome guy ever! He wants to help. We WANT his help!

Fred also has a theory. He thinks the masked madman is Krei! Don't know about that. Doesn't matter who he is (she is?). He's going DOWN.

WE ARE READY TO FIGHT!

I am going to design updated gear for EVERYONE. They all have awesome tech already, but I can make them EVEN better. I know I can! I can't wait to get started! I'm starting RIGHT NOW.

Just found out
BAYMAX SCANNED
THE MASKED MAN!
Amazing. Now, Baymax
can locate him anywhere!

WE ARE COMING
FOR YOU masked man.
WATCH. YOUR. BACK.

I am reserving the next
pages for my inventions.

TOP SECRET!

Fred and Baymax are both helping me a lot.
I have tons of work, Not tons of time.
The longer we wait, the more microbots Mr.
Freaky Face is making.
   Baymax is helping me figure out everyone's
height, weight, and other measurements. By
studying and understanding the inventions they
all created at SFIT, I am able to figure out
more about this team's skill sets. Fred is making
sure all the suits are ultra-cool looking!

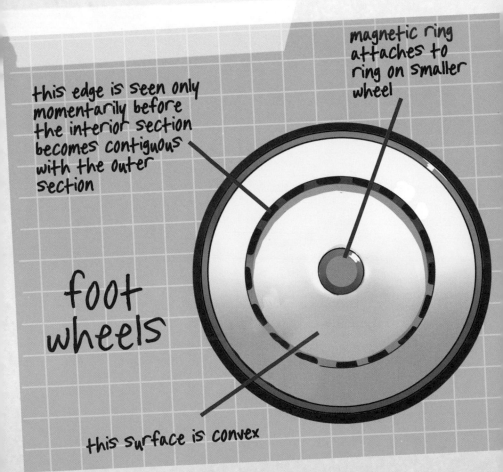

magnetic ring
attaches to
ring on smaller
wheel

this edge is seen only
momentarily before
the interior section
becomes contiguous
with the outer
section

foot
wheels

this surface is convex

Go Go likes speed,
and she ~~likes~~
LOVES wheels.
I can work with that.

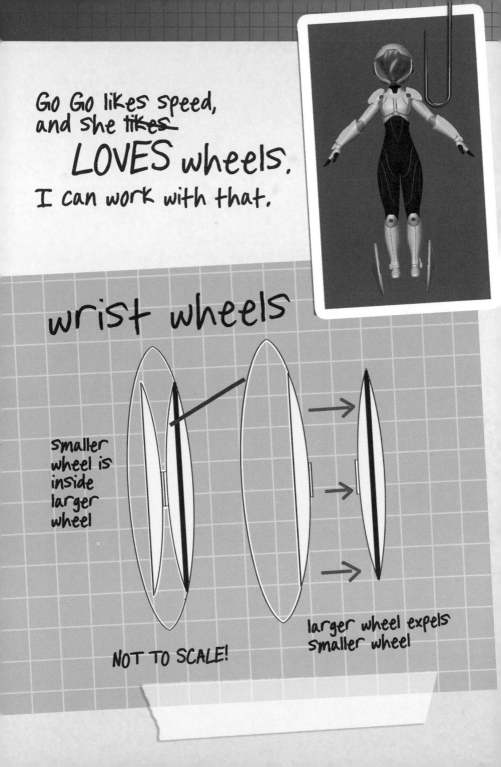

wrist wheels

smaller
wheel is
inside
larger
wheel

NOT TO SCALE!

larger wheel expels
smaller wheel

Go Go's gonna FREAK when she sees this!

yellow areas are thicker armor

discs can also be used as shields or throwing weapons

each ankle has a magnet attachment

electromagnetic discs attach at ankles to act as wheels

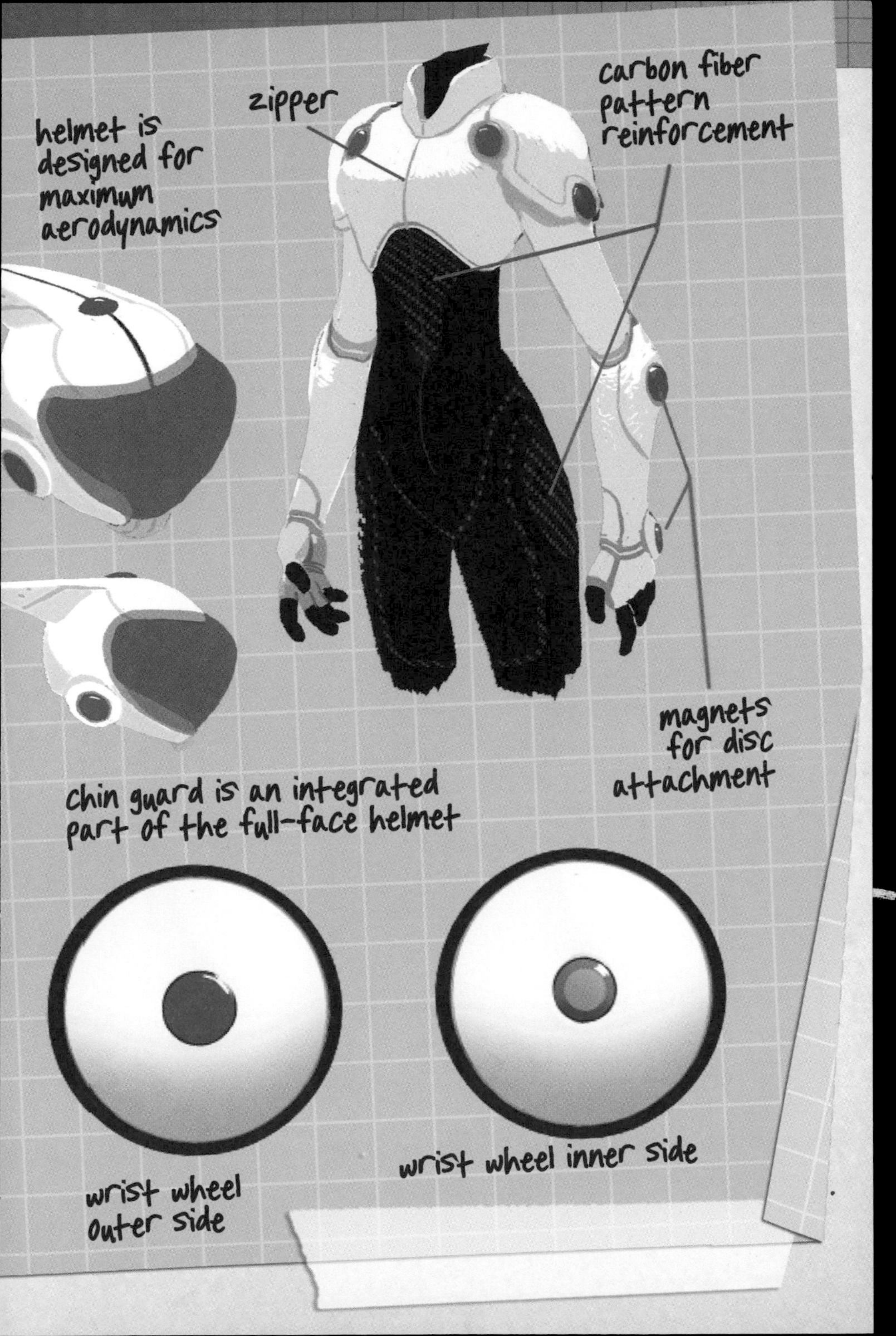

helmet is designed for maximum aerodynamics

zipper

carbon fiber pattern reinforcement

magnets for disc attachment

chin guard is an integrated part of the full-face helmet

wrist wheel outer side

wrist wheel inner side

For Wasabi, I need precision. That dude is precise. Systematic. He's in love with his pinpoint laser.

UPDATE: Here are all the ideas I thought of. I think I will focus on the one-handed plasma blade design. It's a winner!

one-handed plasma ball

creating a ball of energy with two hands

throwing a plasma ball, two hands

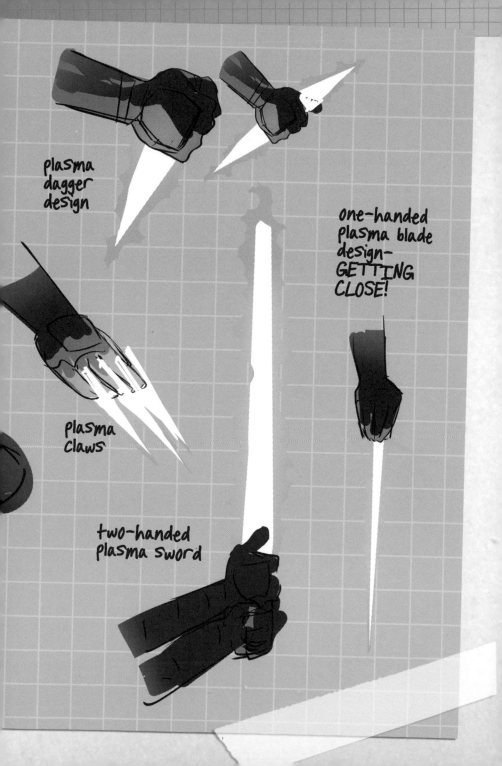

plasma
dagger
design

one-handed
plasma blade
design-
GETTING
CLOSE!

plasma
claws

two-handed
plasma sword

plasma blade
comes out of
the shield on
TOP of the
forearm

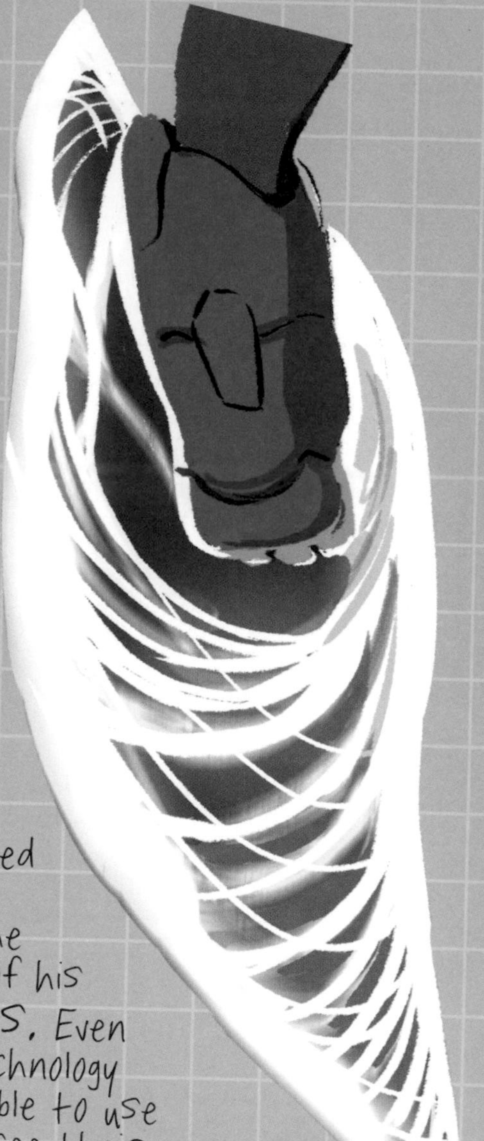

wow!

Today I watched
wasabi start
working with the
early versions of his
plasma gloves. Even
without the technology
in place, he is able to use
the gloves and see their
potential! I can't wait to finish
the upgrades. I am getting pretty
psyched. It's almost like we are...
superheroes!

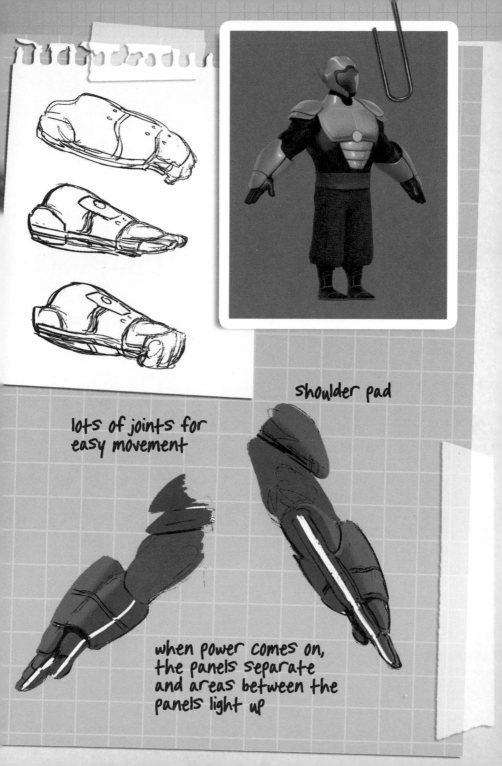

shoulder pad

lots of joints for easy movement

when power comes on, the panels separate and areas between the panels light up

Honey has all the chemistry knowledge she needs. I just have to find a way for her to get **fast** and easy access to the chemicals she wants. Oh, and her gear needs to have colors—like pink. **YUCK!!!** But, hey, she's a girl. And she likes fashion.

Fashion...that's it! A PURSE. A deadly chemical purse! **GENIUS!**

colorful, just like Honey!

Cute, but DEADLY!!

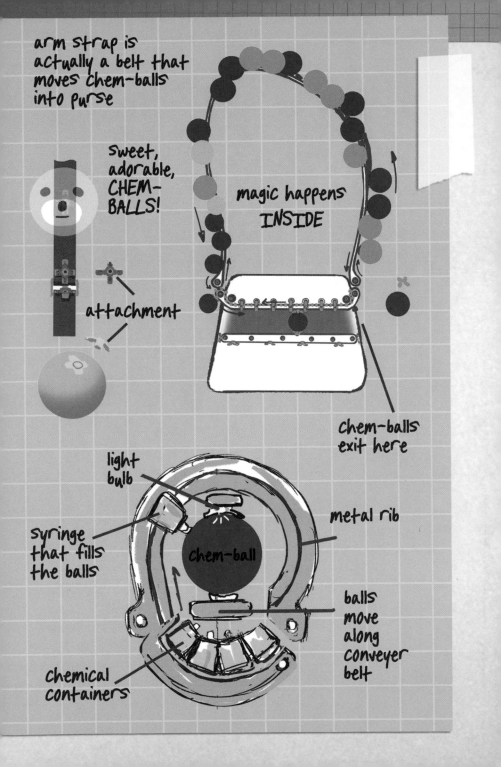

Okay. Fred is harder than the others. I just can't figure out his talent — or anything that he can do well that will help us.

I am going to start with:

1) His love of Kaijus which means monsters in Japanese.
2) His love of comics and superheroes
3) He really wants to be able to superjump.

I GOT IT! Check out Fred's new costume! It makes him look super scary, allows him to super jump, and it can BREATHE FIRE.

Regular Fred is now fire-breathing Fred!

with scary head on

with scary head tipped back

Like in everyone else's suit, Kaiju's head is outfitted with capability for integrated communication

suit is made of flame-resistant material

flamethrower is installed behind mouth

suit allows for superjump maneuvers

I hope he is careful with this thing!!!

Baymax was built with a lot of power. Tadashi told me that he could lift 1,000 pounds! I am going to use that power in Baymax's upgrades:
New armor
More power in his punches
More power in his kicks
Oh, and he will FLY.

I need to add wings and thrusters.

foot thrusters

wings fully extended

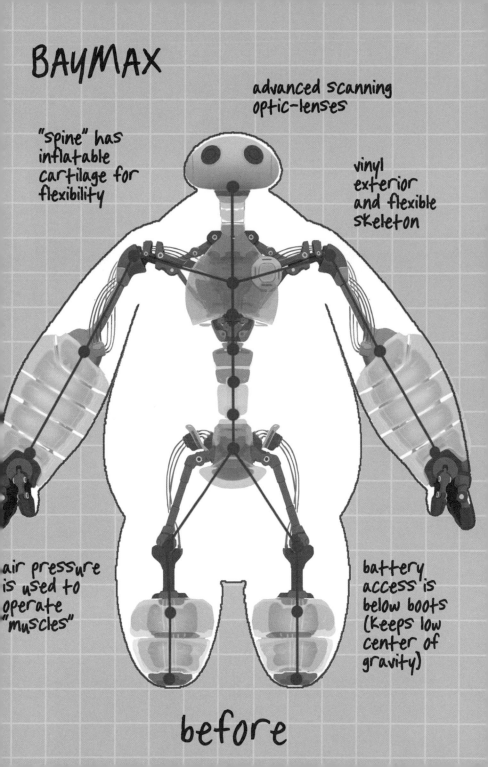

The ideas keep coming...I'm on FIRE!

I added rocket thrusters to Baymax's boots and hands and installed a super scanning device.

Sounds crazy, I know.

forearm opens

glove has fully articulated fingers

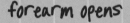

booster retracts into hand area before launch to make room for the actual hand

wrist opening

1

His hands will shoot
right off his arms
to hit a target.
Then, using GPS
tech, RETURN
back to his arms.
We are almost
ready!!! I can
taste victory!

2

3

fins pop out
of glove when
activated

fins allow
rocket to spin
as it leaves
the wrist

Now for me!

I made a list of everything I need: suit, helmet, ~~boots~~ shoes. Big boots are heavy. Sneakers are light and easy to move in—and far cooler.

magnets are mounted on toes of sneakers

It gets better.

I am placing heavy-duty magnets in my gloves and knee pads! If they work, I'll be able to fly on Baymax's back! I'll have a good grip because of the magnets.

I CAN'T WAIT!

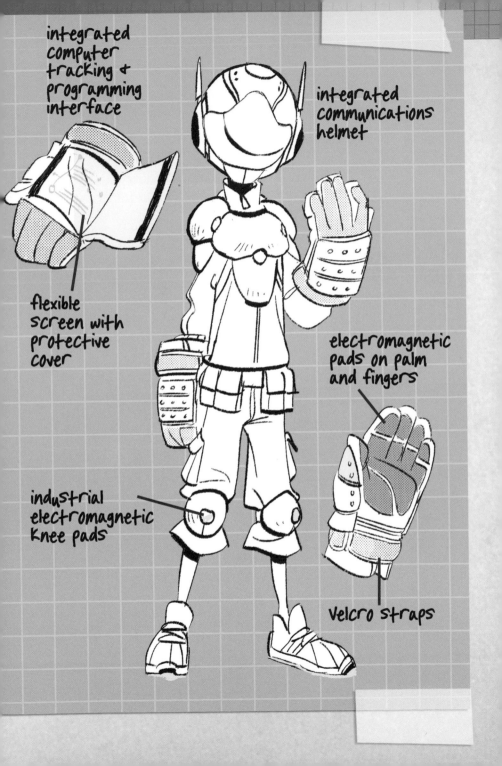

Practice makes perfect.
Good thing because we are far from being perfect. Pretty bad, actually.
My inventions are working fine. Everyone just needs to learn to control ~~there~~, ~~they're~~, their (why is English so hard?) immense power. It's like going from 50 mph to 500 mph. Yeah, it's fun.

But dangerous!

Thank goodness for Heathcliff! Fred's butler helped to clean up the damage we did to Fred's yard! Speaking of which. I need to keep a list of things we've broken so we can replace them.

Small boost to begin rotation.

Rotation rolls over shoulder. NOT a front flip!

Today was the
BEST DAY OF MY LIFE
(so far).

I. FLEW.

No kidding!!!
Today, I FLEW!

This is so awesome!
I wasn't sure if Baymax
was ready, but he **WAS!**

Okay, so Baymax is definitely
good to fly with no problems. With my
electromagnetic gloves and knee
pads, I was able to fly with him. I
just latched onto his back, and
helped navigate.
WE FLEW OVER THE
ENTIRE CITY!

I was screaming and yelling—and it
felt wonderful. Baymax noticed...in
his strange robotic way. Apparently my
"dopamine levels" were way up.
He can be weird, but I'm so happy
I have him.

what do you know? Baymax's super scanner came in MEGA handy. He used it to scan the WHOLE CITY at once! Now we know how to find Yokai. He is not located in the city. He is actually on Akuma Island, an island off the coast. We are about to leave. Baymax will fly us over there. We know this guy is dangerous. I know he has an army of microbots. But I also know we can win this.

N

S

AKUMA ISLAND

Tadashi, I am going to make you proud, brother. I wish you could see us now. We are a team! An awesome team!

I hope everything works out...
if I'm lucky, this won't be
the last entry in this journal!

I am REALLY looking
forward to writing about our
overwhelming success!

OLD
MILITARY
BASE

Well, I'm back home.
And I'm alive.

AND I'M SO ANGRY.

What I said on the last page?
FORGET IT.
Things did NOT work out.
I wasn't lucky.
And somehow I am still here to write.
It was a crazy day. An insane day.
I need to get it out.
To stop from shouting or
hitting something.

So, we snuck onto Akuma Island.
Man, that place is creepy—perfect place
for a bad guy to hang out. The place
was a mess...rubble and broken stuff
everywhere. There were signs of high
tech, top-secret tests there, but the
military closed it down a long time ago.
So, if someone is working there, then the
work is unauthorized.

Well, we KNEW someone was there...
Yokai. And I have to admit. It really
looked like Krei was the one behind the
mask. ESPECIALLY after we saw the
security video.

The video was HORRIFYING. Krei
presented a new invention—a teleportation
portal. On the video, you can see his test
pilot—some girl—flying in. But then, things
went bad. Something went wrong and the device
was destroyed...with the girl still inside.
It was terrible! It makes me sick
thinking about it.

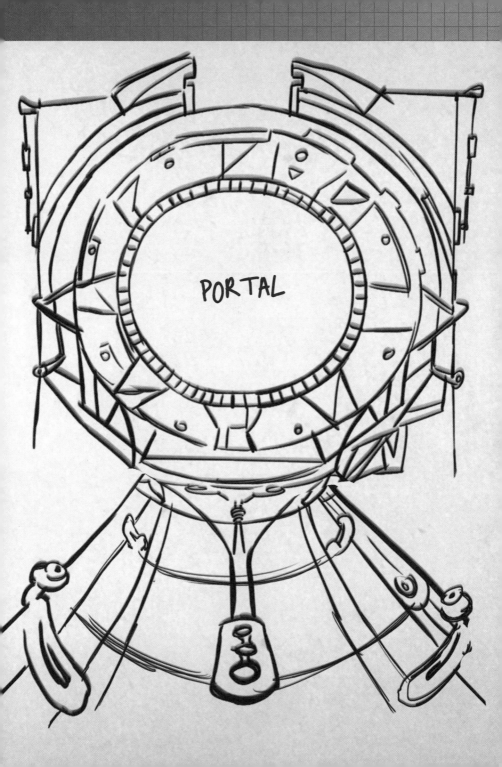

Guess who showed up just as we finished watching the video. Yokai.
Guess what he had with him.

My microbots.

He seemed pretty angry that we were there, all up in his business.
He attacked with the microbots.

And we almost didn't survive. Again.
We were so disorganized.
   But in the scuffle, Yokai's mask was
knocked off. That's when we all saw it
wasn't Krei...but Callaghan. My idol.
The guy I looked up to.
Tadashi's favorite teacher.

Okay, I admit.
I went NUTS.

But, HOW COULD
CALLAGHAN
DO THIS?
HOW?!?!?!!?

  I ripped out Baymax's nurse chip, leaving only the fighting chip I programmed inside. I gave Baymax the order to destroy Callaghan. He was just about to do it.

  We were about to WIN.
  But then, my so-called "friends" stopped Baymax and put the nurse chip back in!!! Callaghan got away.
I'M SO ANGRY. They Knew how important this mission was to me.

  I'm never talking to them again.
  But what do I do now?
  It doesn't matter.

I DON'T
NEED
THEM.

I have the garage all to myself without them around. So, my first order of business is fixing Baymax's scanner. It must have gotten damaged in the fight. At least I can work in peace. Now to take out that nurse chip....

Change of plans....

Baymax showed me some things today. And now I understand. I am so ashamed.

Baymax wouldn't let me open his access port to take out the nurse chip. I was getting pretty frustrated with him. Then he pointed to his chest and my brother appeared.

Tadashi made videos the whole time he was working on Baymax. At the end, he was so proud that he made something that could help people—to heal, not hurt. He would be heartbroken to know I tried to use him to harm someone.

I've been a big jerk.

Good thing I have amazing friends. They forgave me.
We still have a job to do...
we're going to go do it!

Another long day. I'm not sure what to write.

It's late.
I'm exhausted.

I will say this: Today was probably the wildest day of my life. I'm happy, sad, sore, tired, confused.

I need sleep.

Sorry, journal, you'll need to wait until morning.

where do I start?

That test pilot in the video? Her name was Abigail, Abigail Callaghan!! Yeah, she was Callaghan's daughter. The professor blamed Krei for Abigail's death. Callaghan has been out to get revenge all this time!

We figured Callaghan was on his way to Krei Tech. We knew there was going to be trouble.

WE HAD TO STOP HIM!!

We watched Callaghan assemble and reactivate the portal to suck Krei and everything Krei had built inside. It was terrifying.

I tried to help Callaghan understand that I knew how he felt and that revenge wouldn't bring his daughter back. He was SO ANGRY. He wouldn't listen!

Callaghan attacked. But this time my friends and I worked together.

This time, we won. We had no time to celebrate. The portal was out of control.

It was going to IMPLODE.

Then Baymax had something to say. He detected life inside the portal.

It was Abigail!

We both knew what we had to do. And we didn't have much time. We rocketed inside.

It was like being in a raging tornado. But we found Abigail! Alive, but very weak. Baymax was about to rocket us home to safety. But something hit Baymax and damaged the thrusters on his feet.

Baymax knew he could save us, but could not save himself. I made the hardest choice of my life. To let Baymax go. I hugged him good-bye. I felt like I was losing my brother all over again.

I grabbed onto Abigail's pod and he fired one of his fist rockets. We were safely pushed out of the portal. Baymax was left behind.

Lost forever. Like Tadashi.

My heart is broken.

R.I.P.
Baymax

It felt like things wouldn't ever get better, but they did! Things are almost back to normal.

I still miss Tadashi and Baymax. A LOT.

I think about them every day. But I know they wouldn't want me to give up on all my dreams.

Speaking of dreams... SFIT is great! I still can't believe I go there! I am working on an amazing project—it's going to change the world. These days, I see Honey, Wasabi, Go Go, and Fred A LOT. I like the idea of all of us working together again.

Class Schedule

Student: Hiro Hamada
Identification Number: 49820
Spring Semester

I CAN'T BELIEVE IT! I really, really, REALLY can't believe it.
HOW COULD I NOT HAVE NOTICED THIS BEFORE??!?

Today, I picked up Baymax's rocket glove... like I've done hundreds of times. And there it was. His nurse chip! He must have pulled it out before sending me out of the portal. It's been HERE all along. WITH ME.

Unbelievable!

I have a new project now. It's time to bring my friend back. And he is going to be better than ever!

I'm going to need
another journal!